with Reading

OCT 15

The Night of the Were-Boy

By Enid Richemont

Illustrated by

Gustavo Mazali

Crabtree Publishing Company

www.crabtreebooks.com

Crabtree Publishing Company
www.crabtreebooks.com
1-800-387-7650

616 Welland Ave.   PMB 59051, 350 Fifth Ave.
St. Catharines, ON   59th Floor,
L2M 5V6   New York, NY 10118

Published by Crabtree Publishing Company in 2016

First published in 2014 by Franklin Watts
(A division of Hachette Children's Books)

Text © Enid Richemont 2014
Illustration © Gustavo Mazali 2014

Series editor: Melanie Palmer
Series advisor: Catherine Glavina
Series designer: Cathryn Gilbert
Editor: Kathy Middleton
**Proofreader and
 notes to adults:** Shannon Welbourn
**Production coordinator and
 Prepress technician:** Ken Wright
Print coordinator: Amy Salter

Printed in the USA/082015/SN20150529

**Library and Archives Canada
Cataloguing in Publication**

Richemont, Enid, author
        The night of the were-boy / Enid Richemont;
Gustavo Mazali, illustrator.

(Race further with reading)
Issued in print and electronic formats.
ISBN 978-0-7787-2087-4 (bound).--
ISBN 978-0-7787-2111-6 (pbk.).--
ISBN 978-1-4271-1669-7 (pdf).--
ISBN 978-1-4271-1661-1 (html)

        I. Mazali, Gustavo, illustrator II. Title.

PZ7.R393Ni 2015   j823'.914   C2015-903142-7
                                  C2015-903143-5

**Library of Congress
Cataloging-in-Publication Data**

CIP available at Libary of Congress

CHAPTER 1
Full Moon

The full moon was drawing patterns
on the kitchen floor. Frankie opened one
eye. Who had switched that light on?
He yawned. Then he stretched and rolled
over, curling his tail around his head.
Moonlight slowly slithered around the rim
of his basket. Frankie stirred and shivered.
Something was wrong.

He uncurled and went to check on his bowl.

His food smelled funny.

His food smelled wrong.

He backed away from the nasty stench.

He lapped up some milk from his yellow saucer instead.

Yuck, thought Frankie. This food tastes funny. No wonder he felt odd. No wonder he felt strange. No wonder his paws were itching and twitching.

He tried licking them better, but all of a sudden they started to grow. They grew, and they grew. "Meeeoow!" howled Frankie.

Out popped ten stubby fingers from his front paws and ten stubby toes from his back paws.

Frankie stared down at them in disbelief. "Hiss-s-s-s-s!" he cried.

Suddenly he itched all over. He quivered, and crackled, and his head shot up higher than the tabletop. Frankie staggered around on his new long back legs. The floor was so far down now, it made him feel dizzy.

And a *word* came jumping out of his new stretchy mouth.

"HELP!" Frankie heard it.

"Meeeoow!" he wailed.

"Help?"

CHAPTER 2
Fingers and Toes

Frankie's owner, Martin, came into the kitchen. He switched on the light. Then his mouth fell open.

"Who are you?" gasped Martin.

"I'm Frankie," wailed Frankie.

"And I'm not well."

Martin frowned at the empty cat basket.

"And where's my cat?"

"I'm your cat," howled Frankie.

But Martin just looked mad.

"What?" he challenged him. "Because you dyed your hair, and you've got no clothes on? Bet you're a burglar! And a cat-napper." Martin backed away. "I'm getting my dad."

Frankie tried to jump into his basket, but he was much too big.

"I *am* your cat," he sniffed, getting up.

"Some cat!" sneered Martin. "With arms? And legs? And fingers and toes?"

He pointed at each part.

"So where are your whiskers?

Where's your tail?"

"Here," said Frankie. "Look!" He tried to show off his tail, but there wasn't any tail. He tried to lick the fur on his tummy.

He spread out his front claws, but saw ten flat fingernails.

He tried to scratch behind his ear with his five stubby toes.

No tail!

No claws!

No whiskers!

"I'm a monster!" shrieked Frankie.

"OH, MEEEOOOW!"

Martin looked even angrier.

"Stop making those ridiculous cat noises,"

he complained. "It's not funny."

Frankie nibbled between his fingers to comfort himself.

"What have you done with my cat?" demanded Martin.

"Nothing," Frankie whimpered. Then he stole a piece of cake from a plate on the table. Perhaps cake would make his tail grow back.

"Bad cat!" said Martin, without thinking.

"You called me a cat!" crowed Frankie.

"Didn't!"

"Yes, you did!"

"Didn't, didn't, didn't!"

protested Martin.

"Did! Did! DID!"

Frankie tried to purr. Then he sidled up

to Martin and lifted up his chin.

"Scratch me there," he said.

"Scratch yourself," growled Martin.

Then Frankie suddenly remembered something. "Butter," he said, and his mouth began to water. "You let me lick it off your fingers when your mom's not looking."

Martin stared at him, wide-eyed.

That was a secret between him and his cat.

CHAPTER 3
The WereBoy

Frankie was beginning to enjoy himself.

Words were more fun than catnip mice.

He played with some more.

"Remember when I got stuck under the

floorboards?" he said. "I was chasing a

spider. Your dad nearly nailed me in."

"You can't be Frankie," cried Martin. "You're just some weird kid." But, he wondered, how could a burglar know about that?

"And your friend's little sister always pulls my tail," Frankie said. That was true, too.

"You haven't got a tail," said Martin weakly.

Suddenly he noticed the big round moon. Could that be it? he wondered. Like in that scary film on TV where the moon makes a man turn into a wolf? Could it work the other way? Had the full moon turned Frankie into something else? Not a wolf, but a boy? He grinned. They called the man a werewolf, he remembered.

Did that make his cat a were-boy?

"I think you might have been turned into

a were-boy," Martin said slowly.

"A what-boy?" asked Frankie.

"A were-boy," said Martin.

"Like a werewolf, you know."

Frankie shook his head.

"No, I don't," he said.

19

"In the story," Martin told him, "this man gets changed into a wolf each time there's a full moon. Then, when the moon goes down, he gets changed back." He pointed. "Well, there's a full moon tonight."

"So what?" Frankie yawned. "I'm a cat."

"Maybe cats can get changed into other

things, too."

Frankie made a face.

"A wolf would be OK," he grumbled.

"I wouldn't mind being a wolf. But who

wants to look like a boy? Yuck!"

Then he suddenly thought of something.

Boys, thought Frankie, may not have fur.

They may not have tails or actual

whiskers, but they are people. And people

own all the tins of cat food. They own

all the cream, butter, and milk.

A were-boy? thought Frankie.

This might actually be fun.

He tried opening the fridge using his new thumb and his four new fingers. Inside was a feast. Frankie drooled. He pulled out a chicken leg and some chocolate and strawberry cheesecake. He dropped them into his bowl.

"I'm cooking," boasted Frankie.

"I've watched your mom, and I know what to do. You just have to stir things and mix things up." So that is just what he did.

Frankie squatted on the floor and began
to eat. "Yuck!" he yelled. "This tastes awful!"
Martin patted his head.

"Poor old Frankie!" He picked up the bowl.

"Come on. Let's clear up this mess, or Mom
will be mad!"

"It's not a mess." Frankie looked hurt. "And
what do you mean, poor Frankie? I'm a boy
now, so I'm just as good as you."

"Only until the moon goes down," Martin reminded him. "After that, you'll be my cat Frankie again."

"So what?" sniffed Frankie. "At least I'll have a tail and all my fur." He looked scornfully at Martin. "Not like some *people* I could mention."

CHAPTER 4
Backyard Intruders

The hair on Frankie's head suddenly stood on end. He looked kind of scary. "Enemy outside," he hissed.

Scared, Martin ran to the window. Then he grinned. "It's only Samson," he said.

"On *my* territory?" spat Frankie.

He tried to wriggle through the cat flap, but his head got stuck. Martin grabbed him by the waist and hauled him back in. He just couldn't stop laughing.

"Silly Frankie," he said.

Frankie squatted on a pile of old newspapers.

"I want to go out," he sulked.

"Well, you can't," said Martin. "Poor Samson! He hasn't done anything to you."

"He's on my territory," growled Frankie.

"It's his wall, too," Martin pointed out.

"Got to go out," said Frankie slyly.

"Got to pee."

"OK. You win," sighed Martin. "But you can't go out like that."

He pulled some jeans and a sweatshirt out of the laundry basket.

"Put these on," he said. Frankie pushed his arms into the legs of the jeans.

He put his feet into the shirt's sleeves.

Martin rearranged his clothes. It took a long time, because Frankie kept wriggling. "Clothes are stupid!" he grumbled. "I'd much rather just have fur."

Martin opened the kitchen door, and they
went out on to the balcony. Instantly
Samson fled, knocking over all of Martin's
mom's flower pots.

"Get lost!" hissed Frankie, showing off.

Then he leapt up onto the wall.

Martin was horrified.

"Get off there!" he shouted.

"It's a long way down.

You'll fall!"

Frankie sniffed. "Cats never fall," he said snootily. "And even if they do, they always land on their feet. Anyway, there's a fox down there..." He gave a bloodcurdling howl and began dancing up and down. "Watch out, Foxie!" he yelled. "I'm a were-boy, and I'm coming to get you!"

Martin grabbed him by the jeans and hauled Frankie back.

"Keep quiet!" he whispered. "You'll wake up the whole building. Anyway, I thought you came out to pee." He pointed. "There's your box. Go on, do it."

Frankie gaped at the cat litter.

"Too small," he grumbled.

"Can't do it in that."

"*Real* boys," teased Martin, "use a toilet."

"What's a toilet?" asked Frankie.

So Martin explained.

"They do it in the *house*?" howled Frankie.
He looked horrified. "Real boys are
so disgusting."

"It'll have to be down in the yard, then."

Martin sighed. "OK, come on."

He took his mom's keys from the hook.
(He'd be in such big trouble if she found
out!) He opened the front door and closed
it quietly. Then he and Frankie ran down
three flights of stairs and into the big yard
everyone in the building shared. Moonlight
glittered on the grass and there were big
black shadows, but Martin wasn't scared.

This is fun, thought Martin. He was out with a were-boy. He was out with his cat. Then Frankie ran off into the bushes. He must be doing his business, Martin guessed.

He waited politely. He waited a long time.

Was Frankie lost? He began to call:

"Frankie! Frankie!"

Suddenly a hand reached out of the

darkness and covered his mouth.

"Pipe down, kid," said a voice.

And it wasn't Frankie's.

CHAPTER 5
Were-Boy to the Rescue

Shining a flashlight in Martin's face, a man whispered, "Where's your little friend?"

A second man grabbed Martin's arm.

"We don't like all this noise," he said.

"We're on an important job." He smiled a nasty smile.

"So where's this kid Frankie?" demanded the first man.

Martin shivered. "I don't know."

Something moved in the bushes.

Something rustled, then stopped.

"What was that?" muttered the first man.

He cast his flashlight around and caught a

glimpse of the jeans Frankie was wearing.

"It must be this kid's friend Frankie."

Frankie was crouching in the ivy.

His shoulders were quivering, and his

eyes glowed bright blue.

"What's he up to?" sneered the man.
"Why is he creeping around like a cat?"
"Frankie, run!" yelled Martin. "Go and
get help!" But Frankie just stiffened—
and stared.

The first man walked up to him slowly.
"We don't like kids creeping around," he said.
"We get nasty," said the second man,
"very nasty."
But Frankie still didn't move. He just stared.

The man tried to grab him. Then Frankie leaped. His striped hair bristled, and his nails were like knives.

"Aaaaagh!" yelped the first man.

The second man gaped as the were-boy struck again. "This kid's an animal!" he screamed. "Let's get out of here!"

The moon began setting behind the buildings. People were coming outside. "What was all that noise about?" people were saying. Martin heard his dad's voice: "What's going on down there?"

And suddenly, down in the bushes, there was a small, gray-and-white cat.

Martin helped little Frankie out of his tangle of clothes. "Told you," he whispered, pointing up at the sky.

Then Frankie snuggled up against Martin's pajamas and put his two front paws against Martin's chest.

A police siren wailed past.

"I hope they catch those two," Martin whispered to Frankie. He quietly unlocked the front door and tiptoed inside. In the kitchen, he put Frankie back into his basket. Then he took a crust of bread and spread butter on it. Frankie sniffed. Something smelled tasty. Martin put the bread down next to his bowl.

"For supercats," he whispered.

"For were-boys. For you."

Frankie wriggled down and came over.

He lapped up some milk. Then he nosed

at his cat food. It smelled quite delicious.

He licked all the butter off the crust of bread.

Then he climbed back inside his basket.

His tummy felt fat, and his whiskers tasted

buttery.

He had been in a fight, he remembered,

yawning. With Samson? He stretched,

then wound his tail around his head.

Whoever it was with, he knew he had won.

It must have been a dream, thought Martin in the morning. He had dreamed that his cat had turned into a boy. Then Mom gasped. "Who made that mess on the kitchen floor?" she demanded. Martin saw the sticky, chocolate trail. He shrugged. "Not me."

"Maybe it was burglars," joked Dad. "They caught a couple in the building's yard last night. Someone heard noises in the bushes and called the police."

"I know," Mom said. "The funny thing is—people say the burglars actually seemed glad to be caught." Grinning, Martin looked down at Frankie and gave him a wink.

Notes for Adults

Race Further with Reading is the next entertaining level up for young readers from **Race Ahead with Reading**. Longer, more in-depth chapters and fun illustrations help children build up their vocabulary and reading skills in a fun way.

THE FOLLOWING BEFORE, DURING, AND AFTER READING ACTIVITY SUGGESTIONS SUPPORT LITERACY SKILL DEVELOPMENT AND CAN ENRICH SHARED READING EXPERIENCES:

BEFORE

1. Make reading fun! Choose a time to read when you and the reader are relaxed and have time to share the story together. Don't forget to give praise! Children learn best in a positive environment.
2. Before reading, ask the reader to look at the title and illustrations on the cover of the book **The Night of the Were-Boy.** Invite them to make predictions about what will happen in the story. They may make use of prior knowledge and make connections to other stories they have heard or read about a similar character.

DURING

3. Encourage readers to determine unfamiliar words themselves by using clues from the text and illustrations.
4. During reading, encourage the child to review his or her understanding and see if they want to revise their predictions midway. Encourage the reader to make text-to-text connections, choosing a part of the story that reminds them of another story they have read; and text-to-self connections, choosing a part of the story that relates to their own personal experiences; and text-to-world connections, choosing a part of the story that reminds them of something that happened in the real world.

AFTER

5. Ask the reader who the main characters are. Describe how the characters' traits or feelings impact the story.
6. Have the child retell the story in their own words. Ask him or her to think about the predictions they made before reading the story. How were they the same or different?

7. Encourage the reader to refer to parts in the story by the chapters the events occurred in and explain how the story developed.

DISCUSSION QUESTIONS FOR KIDS

8. Martin shows various emotions as he comes to realize that his pet cat, Frankie, is the were-boy, not an intruder. Discuss the different emotions and responses Martin has throughout this story.
9. Choose one of the illustrations from the story. How do the details in the picture help you understand a part of the story better? Or, what do the illustrations tell you that is not in the text?
10. What part of the story surprised you? Why was it a surprise?
11. From your point of view, and before Martin figured out that the full moon had caused Frankie to change into a were-boy, what did you think had happened to Frankie the cat to make him change?
12. What moral, or lesson, can you take from this story?
13. Create your own story or drawing about a pet or animal you wish could walk and talk like a human.
14. Have you read another story by the same author? Compare the stories you have read by the same author or compare this story to other books in the **Race Further with Reading** series.
15. If you had a pet, what do you think it would say to you?